OTHER HISTORY BOOKS

Kings, queens, explorers, authors, famous women –
here is social history at its best, for school use or simply to enjoy.

Series 561

GREAT RULERS

Alexander the Great

Julius Caesar and Roman
Britain

Cleopatra and Ancient Egypt

King Alfred the Great

William the Conqueror

King John and Magna Carta

Robert the Bruce

Richard the Lion Heart

Henry V

Henry VIII

First Queen Elizabeth

Oliver Cromwell

Napoleon

Queen Victoria

Kings and Queens (Book 1)

Kings and Queens (Book 2)

GREAT AUTHORS

Charles Dickens

William Shakespeare

PREHISTORY

Stone Age Man in Britain

GREAT EXPLORERS

Christopher Columbus

Captain Cook

Sir Francis Drake

David Livingstone

Marco Polo

Captain Scott

GREAT MEN

Bonnie Prince Charlie

Nelson

Pilgrim Fathers

John Wesley

GREAT WOMEN

Joan of Arc

Florence Nightingale

GREAT CIVILISATIONS

The Aztecs

China

Crete

Egypt

Greece

The Incas

The Mycenaeans

Rome

The Vikings

CONTENTS

		page
	Introduction	4
871-899	Alfred the Great	6
899-924	Edward the Elder	8
924-939	Aethelstan	9
939-946	Edmund the Elder	9
946-955	Edred	9
955-959	Edwy	9
959-975	Edgar the Peaceful	10
975-978	Edward the Martyr	13
978-1016	Aethelred the Unready	13
1016	Edmund Ironside	13
1016-1035	Canute	14
1035-1040	Harold I	15
1040-1042	Hardecanute	15
1042-1066	Edward the Confessor	16
1066	Harold II	18
1066-1087	William the Conqueror	19
1087-1100	William II (Rufus)	20

		page
1100-1135	Henry I, known as Beauclerc	24
1135-1154	Stephen	26
1154-1189	Henry II	28
1189-1199	Richard I	30
1199-1216	John, nicknamed Lackland	32
1216-1272	Henry III	34
1272-1307	Edward I, nicknamed Longshanks	36
1307-1327	Edward II	38
1327-1377	Edward III	40
1377-1399	Richard II	42
1399-1413	Henry IV	44
1413-1422	Henry V	46
1422-1461 and 1470-1471	Henry VI	47
1461-1470 and 1471-1483	Edward IV	49
1483	Edward V	50
1483-1485	Richard III	50
	Lines of descent	Back endpaper

Acknowledgment:
The photograph on page 35 is by John Moyes.

Revised edition
Published by Ladybird Books Ltd Loughborough Leicestershire UK
Ladybird Books Inc Lewiston Maine 04240 USA

Book 1

Kings and Queens
of England

written by BRENDA RALPH LEWIS
illustrated by JOHN LEIGH-PEMBERTON
and PETER ROBINSON

Ladybird Books

Invading Vikings fight with Anglo-Saxons

Before the Kings and Queens

People have always had leaders and, eventually, leaders have always acquired titles. In time, the families of many of these leaders became *ruling* or *royal* families. In fact, the origin of the title, *king*, came from the Anglo-Saxon, *cyning*, meaning kin or family.

The first kings in Britain were really more like local chieftains ruling over tribes, living in clearings in the mass of forest that smothered most of the land. By the time the Romans invaded (43 AD), some tribes were very large, and historians described their chiefs as *Cunobelin, King of the Trinovantes* (Colchester) or *Boadicea (Boudicca), Queen of the Iceni* (East Anglia).

However, many centuries passed before there were kings of all England, and they arose from the vigorous, warlike invaders who first raided the coasts of Roman Britain in the 3rd century AD. They were the Anglo-Saxons, i.e. Angles, Jutes and Saxons from northern Germany and Denmark. After 426 AD, when the Romans had abandoned Britain, the Anglo-Saxons invaded in ever-increasing numbers. They drove the inhabitants westwards, towards Wales, and carved out their own kingdoms; Northumbria, Mercia, Wessex and East

Anglia, among them.

Then in the 8th century, history began to repeat itself. It became the turn of the Anglo-Saxons to face fierce foreign invaders: the Vikings from Scandinavia. Within a century, the Vikings occupied vast areas of England, and only the Anglo-Saxon kings of Wessex remained to challenge them.

Because the challenge succeeded, this is where the story of the kings and queens of England begins.

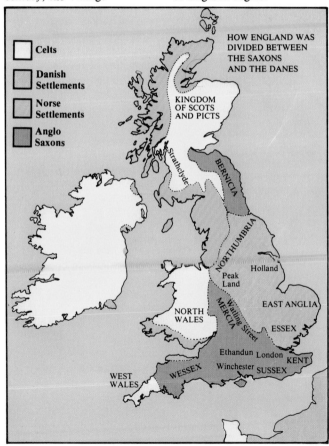

Celts

Danish Settlements

Norse Settlements

Anglo Saxons

HOW ENGLAND WAS DIVIDED BETWEEN THE SAXONS AND THE DANES

KINGDOM OF SCOTS AND PICTS

Strathclyde

BERNICIA

NORTHUMBRIA

Holland

Peak Land

NORTH WALES

MERCIA

Watling Street

EAST ANGLIA

ESSEX

Ethandun London

Winchester

KENT

SUSSEX

WESSEX

WEST WALES

THE SAXON KINGS
Alfred the Great – 871-899 AD

Saxon nobles wore their hair shoulder length. Moustaches were long and beards forked

The royal family of Wessex was a family of warriors, and

Alfred, the last of four brothers to rule the kingdom in the 9th century, fought the Danish Viking invaders nine times in 871, the year he came to the throne. At this time, the Danes occupied one half of England and had their greedy eyes on the other half: the territory of Wessex. To stop them, Alfred built fortresses and formed a new navy, and he organised his army so that one half guarded the kingdom while the other farmed the land.

Nevertheless, in 877, a Danish army managed to break in and attack Alfred's palace at Chippenham. Alfred fled to the Athelney marshes (Somerset).

Alfred built fortresses and formed new armies to protect the kingdom

Other Anglo-Saxon kings, in similar situations, had given up in despair or tried to bribe the Danes to go away, but not Alfred. In 878, he burst out of hiding and gave the Danes such a thrashing that their leader, Guthrum, promised never to invade Wessex again.

Alfred used the peace he had won to concentrate on his work of founding schools to improve education, and restoring monasteries to invigorate religious life. Famous scholars came to Alfred's court at Winchester to help him to translate from Latin the first books to be written in the English language. Alfred also had the chance now to frame laws and so civilise his subjects.

The most important law was, 'Do not to others what you would not have them do to you'. This remarkable combination of warrior and scholar earned Alfred the title, 'the Great', a title not bestowed on any other king in England.

Alfred was a great scholar and translated books from Latin into English

7

**The family of Alfred
the Great – 899-1017:
Edward the Elder – 899-924
Aethelstan – 924-939
Edmund the Elder – 939-946
Edred – 946-955
Edwy – 955-959**

England was extremely
fortunate that the first kings
after Alfred were, like him,
men of great ability and
vigour. Alfred's successor, his
son, Edward the Elder
(899-924), spent most of his
reign fighting to push back
the frontiers of the Danelaw,
as the Danish-occupied region
of England was called.

Edward was aided during
917-918 by his sister
Ethelfleda, Lady of English
Mercia. Ethelfleda was a
formidable warrior. Even the
Danes were frightened when
they saw her, armour-clad,
sword in hand, leading her
forces into battle. By 918,
Ethelfleda and Edward
controlled all England south
of the River Mersey and the
Humber, and most of the
Danelaw had disappeared.

After Ethelfleda died in 918,
followed by Edward in 924,
Edward's three sons
continued where Ethelfleda
and their father had left off.

Ethelfleda was a formidable warrior

Both Saxons and Danes went into battle on horseback although most of the fighting was done on foot

The eldest, the handsome and impressive King Aethelstan (924-939), pushed the Danes even further northwards, destroyed the new Danish kingdom of York, and formed England into roughly the area it occupies today. Aethelstan's brothers, Edmund (939-946) and Edred (946-955) spent their years as kings strengthening the gains Aethelstan had made.

Their nephew, Edwy, who became king in 955 aged about 15 and died four years later, had little chance to make his mark upon the history of England. Edwy did however quarrel with Dunstan, Bishop of London, by leaving his coronation to visit his future bride and her mother. Dunstan, it seems, went after the teenage king and dragged him back to the coronation feast. Dunstan was later forced to leave England but soon returned, after English nobles tired of the feckless Edwy. They chose his younger brother, Edgar, as king instead in 959.

Edwy quarrels with the Bishop of London at the coronation feast

9

Edgar the Peaceful – 959-975

It was a brilliant choice, for King Edgar was a true heir of Alfred the Great. He was also the first king since Alfred who did not have to spend time and effort fighting wars. His uncles, Áethelstan, Edmund and Edred had seen to that.

Together with Dunstan, the young King Edgar, who was only thirteen when he came to the throne, turned his attention to furthering the education and revival of religious life which Alfred the

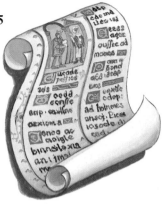

Illuminated manuscript

Great had begun. Their work was very fruitful. Some of the most beautiful illuminated

Monks distributing charity

manuscripts ever produced in England date from Edgar's time, and so does the building of beautiful abbeys filled with stained-glass windows. This was a 'golden age' of learning and strict religious observance, when more scholarly books were translated into English and monks began to lead worthier and more dedicated lives.

By 973, Edgar's prestige was so great that, as tradition has it, he was rowed across the River Dee by six kings. This act of humility on their part showed how wholeheartedly they accepted Edgar as their overlord.

A Saxon ship

11

A Saxon tower built of stone. The windows were arches with a rounded top

That same year, Edgar was crowned in Bath Abbey in a coronation ceremony which, in its essentials, remains the same today. The most important part of it, the anointing of the monarch's head with holy oil, came to be seen as something which set kings and queens apart from ordinary folk. It established the idea that there was a special *magic* in kingship, a magic conferred directly by God.

The coronation of Edgar

Edward the Martyr – 975-978
Aethelred the Unready – 978-1016
Edmund Ironside – 1016

Tragically this 'golden age' ended abruptly with Edgar's death two years later in 975. From then onwards, a shadow fell across the Anglo-Saxon monarchy and deepened as time went on. Edgar's son and successor, Edward, was murdered in 978, aged 16. The culprit, apparently, was his stepmother, who wanted her own son, Aethelred, aged 10, to be king instead. She got her wish and brought disaster upon England.

Aethelred well deserved his nickname 'the Unready', meaning 'ill-advised'. Under his weak rule, England was swamped year after year by new Danish invaders who left a trail of slaughter, destruction, sorrow and terror behind them. In 1003, King Sweyn of Denmark drove Aethelred into exile in Normandy, and was acclaimed king of England. After Sweyn died in 1014, the English nobles invited Aethelred to come back, as long as he ruled more competently. Sweyn however had a son, Canute, and he was not going to let England go that easily. In 1015, Canute brought a great invasion fleet to Kent and devastating warfare resumed. After King Aethelred died in April 1016, his son and successor, Edmund Ironside, carried on the struggle against the Danes. Edmund proved so mighty a warrior that Canute agreed to share England with him. It never happened. Edmund died suddenly in November 1016 (he may have been murdered) and Canute came into possession of all England.

BREAKING UP SOIL – DIGGING – SOWING – HARROWING
Country life as depicted in the Anglo-Saxon calendar

13

King Canute – 1016-1035 and his sons

Canute was a man of extensive power. He collected no less than three kingdoms; England (1017), Denmark (1019) and Norway (1028). It took intrigue and brute force for Canute to get his hands on Norway, but it was well worth it. Norway brought under Canute's rule a vast swathe of territory, stretching from the Isle of Man to Greenland. It was an empire, and one which Canute ruthlessly guarded against all rivals. For instance, he sent two of Edmund Ironside's sons to remote Hungary, doubtless hoping that they would never return.

Canute however was no puffed up barbarian, over-confident of his power. He knew there were limitations to what one man could do. Though he kept England in good order and was a devout, conscientious Christian, Canute realised that once he was dead, his squabbling relatives and nobles would not keep his three kingdoms together nor rule them well.

Canute's courtiers had said that the sea would obey him. So Canute ordered back the sea and got very wet proving how stupid were their flatteries

Harold I (Harefoot) – 1035-1040
Hardecanute – 1040-1042

Canute was right. Unrest and insecurity followed his death in 1035, for he was succeeded in England by his worthless sons, Harold Harefoot (1035-1040) and Hardecanute (1040-1042). Neither was a competent king and Hardecanute was a thoroughgoing ruffian. His dreadful deeds included digging up his brother's body and flinging it into a fen, and probably conniving at the murder of one of his nobles. When Hardecanute died, apparently of too much drink, the English joyously welcomed his successor, particularly as he belonged to their own royal family of Wessex. He was another son of King Aethelred the Unready, Edward, afterwards known to history as Edward the Confessor.

Edward the Confessor

15

King Edward the Confessor – 1042-1066

Edward was the last Anglo-Saxon king of the English and was made a Saint in 1161

Edward the Confessor is usually depicted as a weak, unworldly king, more interested in religion than in ruling his country. Monks wrote that he lived 'like an angel in the squalor of the world'. Edward was sincerely religious and peaceloving, but he was no angel. When he became king in 1042, after 25 years of exile in Normandy, he was very determined to preserve his power.

In 1051, for instance, Earl Godwin of Wessex tried to bully Edward and gathered an army against him. Edward refused to yield to the Earl's demands, and eventually sent the Godwin family into exile. In 1052, Edward ordered the murder of the Welsh Prince, Rhys, as punishment for Welsh terror raids into England. Afterwards, when Rhys' head was brought to him, Edward did not even wince at the grisly sight. These were not the acts of a weak king.

Saxon costume
Sleeves and leggings were very full and gathered in for extra warmth

Furthermore, England was relatively peaceful during Edward's reign; not the sort of thing a weak ruler normally achieved. Evidence lies in the fact that the hiding of money hoards, a sure sign of insecure times, dropped dramatically while he was king.

Of course, Edward made his mistakes, and he angered his English subjects by giving important posts to his Norman friends. Edward's most dreadful mistake, however, was to offer his crown, first in 1052 to his cousin Duke William of Normandy, and later, when the quarrel with the Godwins was mended, to Harold, Earl Godwin's son.

The result was catastrophic – nothing less than the end of Anglo-Saxon England.

The first Westminster Abbey built by Edward as shown in the Bayeux tapestry. Made about 1070 the tapestry is in the form of a strip cartoon and tells the story of King Harold and William the Conqueror and the events that led to the Battle of Hastings in 1066. The pictures are embroidered on linen. It is 230 feet long and the crooked lines and leaning tower of the abbey are partly due to the shrinkage and stretching of the ancient material during the last nine hundred years

Harold II (Godwinson) – 1066

Harold Godwinson, elected king by the Witan (royal council) after Edward the Confessor died (January 1066), never had a chance to prove himself as a ruler. Although he was an accomplished soldier, even his military skills could not deal with the situation in England the following autumn when he was invaded by two rivals with large, powerful armies. One belonged to Harald Hardrada (*hard ruler*), King of Norway, who intended to reclaim the throne that had once belonged to Canute. Harold Godwinson defeated and killed Hardrada at Stamford Bridge (September), but then had to march 402 km southwards to meet the invading army of William of Normandy. William, furious at being cheated of the throne Edward the Confessor promised him, fought and killed the exhausted Harold at Hastings (October), and so ended Anglo-Saxon rule in England.

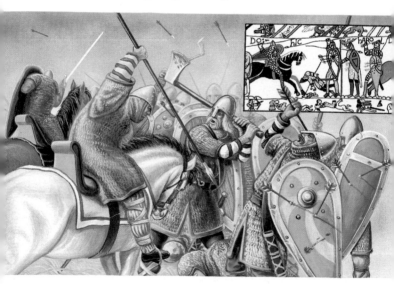

Harold was killed by William at the Battle of Hastings in 1066. Inset shows detail of the Bayeux tapestry ordered by Bishop Odo, half-brother of William I

THE NORMANS
William the Conqueror – 1066-1087

Normans wore their hair short and were clean shaven

As William I 'the Conqueror', he governed England, as he governed Normandy, by one simple rule: William was generous to those who obeyed him and ruthless to those who did not. He tried, at first, to gain the co-operation of the conquered English. When this failed, English rebellions were brutally punished. A rising in the North resulted in devastation. Crops and villages were burned and cattle and people slaughtered. Meanwhile Norman barons replaced Saxon nobles. The people became *villeins* under the *feudal system,* which bound them to their Norman lords almost like slaves. For taxation purposes, a list was made of all the land, buildings and cattle in England. This was called the Domesday Book.

In the forests, now largely royal territory, the English were forbidden to kill the game birds they had relied on for food.

No wonder they found William's conquest a painful, humiliating experience.

A Norman Castle: William built many castles including the White Tower of the Tower of London

The sons of William the Conqueror:
William II (Rufus) – 1087-1100
Robert

William the Conqueror's sons soon proved a troublesome, quarrelsome lot after their father died in 1087. The easygoing, but lazy Robert, called Curthose because of his short legs, became Duke of Normandy.

Norman cavalry was the deciding factor in many battles

England went to the second surviving son, who became King William II. He was called Rufus because of his red face and bad temper. Richard, the second son, had been killed while hunting in 1081. The youngest son, Henry, who was left £5,000 in silver, was cunning, greedy and faithless. When Robert and William quarrelled, Henry sided with each of them in turn.

William Rufus was soon plotting to get Normandy away from Robert. By 1096,

Norman Man at Arms: his coat was called a hauberk and was made of leather with metal studs. It had a hood to go over the head called a coif. The helmet had a piece to protect the nose. Under the hauberk the man would wear a linen tunic. The shoes were leather and his legs were covered with woollen stockings called chausses

he had succeeded, by a mixture of bribery and brute force. William paid Robert's barons to desert him and then invaded Normandy, and eventually Robert was only too glad to escape from him. He pawned Normandy to William for 10,000 marks and set off on a Crusade to the Holy Land.

By this time, the English had already discovered that William Rufus was a harsh ruler *all* the time, unlike his father, who knew when to be merciful.

Preparations for William's invasion of Normandy

After 1095, rebellions in Northumberland, Wales and Scotland were put down with great savagery and slaughter. Unlike William the Conqueror, who had been a devout Christian, Rufus cared nothing for the Church or for God. The blasphemies he uttered were enough to make monks faint with shock, and in their chronicles, they wrote of their Godless King with horror. William looked on the Church, however, as a very useful source of income, to add to the very heavy taxes he imposed on his subjects. He used to keep Church posts vacant for long periods of time and pocket the revenues. Only once was William Rufus frightened enough to pay heed to religion. That was in 1093, when he fell ill and thought he was dying. To save himself, or so it seems,

Rufus appointed the saintly Anselm as Archbishop of Canterbury. King and Archbishop soon quarrelled. Anselm believed the Pope's power in England should be greater than the King's. William believed the opposite. Neither would give in and eventually Anselm left England in despair (1097). Then suddenly, and monks thought deservedly, William was struck by disaster. On 2nd August 1100, he was mysteriously killed by an arrow while hunting in the New Forest. Was it an accident or was it murder? And if it was murder, was

William's death

Henry seizes the royal treasury

Henry the man responsible? Henry, as it happens, was also hunting in the New Forest when William was killed and afterwards he acted as if he was prepared for it to happen. As soon as he heard his brother was dead, Henry rode at top speed to seize the royal treasury at Winchester. On 5th August 1100, he was crowned King Henry I in Westminster Abbey.

Soon afterwards Robert arrived home from crusading to find Henry waiting with an army to challenge him for Normandy. After several years of warfare and intrigue, Henry smashed Robert's army at the battle of Tinchebrai in 1106. Robert spent the rest of his life, 28 years, in prison.

The Battle of Tinchebrai

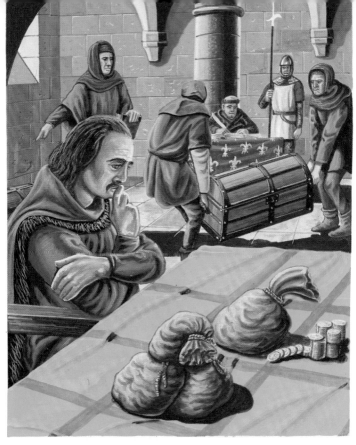

Counting taxes on a chequerboard. This is the origin of the word 'exchequer'

King Henry I, known as Beauclerc – 1100-1135

King Henry I was nasty, greedy, cruel, and treacherous towards his brothers. Yet men like this often made suitable kings in violent, medieval times; kings who could make their subjects feel the sharp edge of their authority. This was something Henry certainly accomplished. He overhauled the taxation system so that sheriffs and other tax collectors found it more difficult to cheat. Taxes were now counted out on a chequerboard and sometimes King Henry watched in person

White Ship disaster in which Henry's son drowned

to see that all the money was there. Henry created the *Curia Regis* (King's Court) to try legal cases, so that fines paid by wrongdoers went to his treasury. Previously local judges had pocketed these fines. All this made the people feel confident that the king was personally concerned that justice should be done and the king's peace kept. The orderly kingdom that resulted was important for Henry, who spent half his reign abroad, fighting successfully to defend Normandy from attack. Then, in 1120, a tragedy endangered Henry's well-ordered kingdom. His son, William, drowned in a shipwreck, leaving Henry with a daughter, Matilda. At a time when kings often had to go to war, a woman was

thought unsuitable to rule. So, although Henry twice made his barons swear allegiance to Matilda as his heir, he had little hope they would keep their word, and all the more so because they loathed Matilda's husband, Count Geoffrey of Anjou. There was going to be trouble, as was soon proved after Henry died in 1135.

Geoffrey of Anjou and Matilda
Geoffrey was only 16 when they married 25

King Stephen – 1135-1154 and The Empress Matilda

Three weeks after Henry I died, England had a new monarch. It was not Matilda, his heir, but Henry's favourite nephew, Stephen of Blois (France). Stephen had crossed to England when he heard Henry was dead and was quickly crowned in Westminster Abbey (22nd December 1135). Proud, wilful Matilda was not to be cheated of her inheritance, so she waged war on Stephen and the barons who supported him.

King David of Scotland, Matilda's uncle, invaded northern England. Her half-brother, Robert, invaded the West Country. Her husband, Geoffrey, made war in

Plan of a Norman village:

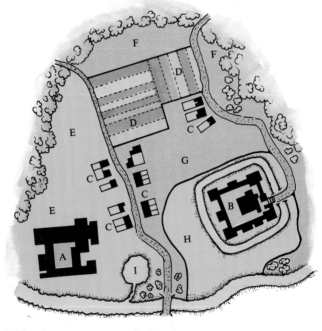

A	Monastery	
B	Castle	
C	Cottages	
D	Arable strips	
E	Common pasture	
F	Waste ground	
G	Open market	
H	Cattle pasture	
I	Fish pond	

Normandy. The barons, freed from King Henry's iron control, enjoyed their own local wars.

Even so, Matilda was not strong enough to defeat Stephen and he was too easygoing to defeat her. In 1139, Stephen's forces captured Matilda but he was too chivalrous to imprison her, and let her go. In 1141, Matilda captured and imprisoned Stephen, and went to London for her coronation. She was so high handed, though, that Londoners became offended and threw her out.

Matilda gave up in 1148, and her son, Henry Plantagenet, carried on the struggle. The Barons in Normandy wanted Henry to be Stephen's heir for they felt, quite rightly,

that Stephen had no interest in Normandy. Stephen wanted his own son, Eustace, to be king after him, but the problem was tragically solved when Eustace suddenly died (1153). Stephen was heartbroken, and agreed that Henry Plantagenet should succeed him.

Henry did not have to wait long. Stephen never recovered from Eustace's death, and died fourteen months later, in October 1154.

Geoffrey of Anjou wore a sprig of broom in his hat. Its Latin name, Planta genista, *gave rise to the nickname,* Plantagenet, *which was adopted by subsequent monarchs*

Farming in Norman times

Oxen were used for ploughing because they worked better than horses over the muddy ground

THE PLANTAGENETS
King Henry II – 1154-1189

During this reign men were clean shaven or wore close cut beards. Hair was curled

When Henry Plantagenet, Duke of Normandy, Count of Anjou and Lord of Aquitaine, was crowned King Henry II (19 December 1154), England became part of his vast empire. The English also acquired just the king they needed; one who could impose law and order after years of anarchy.

Fiery-tempered, restless and energetic, Henry II firmly believed in well-organised government and efficient lawcourts. In the courts, Henry abolished the barbarous 'trial by ordeal', in which people plunged their hands into boiling water or grasped red-hot iron bars to prove their innocence. In Henry's lawcourts, decisions were made by judges who heard evidence from twelve 'jurymen'.

To Henry's fury, however, the Church refused to let priests be judged in his courts. To solve the problem, Henry created his closest friend, Thomas Becket, Archbishop of Canterbury in 1162. Unexpectedly, Becket fiercely defended the Church's rights to its own lawcourts. Tragedy followed when four of the enraged Henry's knights murdered Becket in Canterbury Cathedral (1170).

Henry's sons also plagued him with troubles. Henry would not share his power with them, so, infuriated, two of them – Richard and

The arms of Stephen (top) and those of Henry II. The three lions have remained on the Royal Coat of Arms ever since

John – joined forces with their father's great enemy, King Philip of France.

In 1189, Richard, John and Philip made war on King Henry, who was very ill at the time. When Henry heard of the treachery of John, his favourite son, he lost heart and acknowledged defeat. Two days later, weeping and lamenting his misfortune, Henry II died at his castle of Chinon (France).

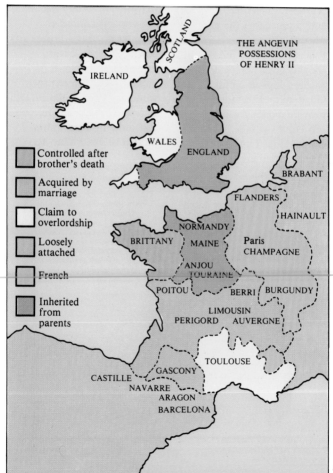

THE ANGEVIN POSSESSIONS OF HENRY II

SCOTLAND

IRELAND

WALES

ENGLAND

BRABANT

FLANDERS

HAINAULT

NORMANDY

BRITTANY   MAINE

Paris

CHAMPAGNE

ANJOU
TOURAINE

POITOU   BERRI   BURGUNDY

LIMOUSIN
PERIGORD   AUVERGNE

TOULOUSE

CASTILLE   GASCONY

NAVARRE

ARAGON

BARCELONA

Controlled after brother's death

Acquired by marriage

Claim to overlordship

Loosely attached

French

Inherited from parents

King Richard I, The Lionheart – 1189-1199

Richard I, who in 1189 succeeded the father he so brutally betrayed, is one of England's most romantic kings. He was a great crusader, chivalrous knight, and 'Lionheart', the mighty warrior.

England however paid dearly for this great hero-king, for Richard looked on his kingdom as a treasurehouse to provide money for his part in the Third Crusade (1189-1192). To this end, Richard virtually put England up for sale. He sold land, manors, sheriffdoms, earldoms, Church and government posts, for cash. Richard even seemed willing to sell the city of London. 'If only I could find someone rich enough to buy it!' he apparently declared.

As a result, Richard went off on the Crusade leaving England in the hands of inexperienced, greedy men who were soon occupied with their own quarrels. Meanwhile Richard's brother, John, plotted to undermine his power.

A 13th century sword. When Richard failed to capture Jerusalem during the third Crusade, he is reputed to have said: 'If my sword cannot take it, my eyes shall not behold it!'

Crusaders wore a red cross on their shields and on linen tunics worn over their armour

Richard imprisoned by Duke Leopold of Austria

'The barons were disturbed,' wrote a chronicler, 'castles were strengthened, towns fortified, ditches dug...' In other words, people were nervous and scared, and only the presence of Richard's mother, Eleanor, and Walter, Archbishop of Lincoln, prevented a serious breakdown of law and order. Richard cost England yet more money in 1194. He had to be ransomed after being imprisoned by Duke Leopold of Austria on his way home from the Crusade. Richard returned to raise more money for more war, this time defending his territories in France. He then departed after two months (May 1194), never to be seen in England again. Richard died in 1199 after an assassination attempt with a poisoned weapon.

Medieval hawking: men flew falcons, peregrines or goshawks while women flew merlins and often rode pillion behind a servant

King John, nicknamed Lackland — 1199-1216

Also nicknamed 'Soft sword' after the loss of Normandy and Anjou

King John, Henry II's youngest son, has always been seen as an evil monster: a treacherous, cruel, greedy man who was fond of torturing his imprisoned enemies or starving them to death.

John deserved much of his terrible reputation, but he was probably painted blacker than he was by the monk-historians of his time. To them, John committed the worst possible sin. He quarrelled with the Pope (1205), and brought on England the dreadful punishment of the Pope's Interdict (1208-1214). This meant that the English were exiled from the Church. Worse still, during the Interdict, John robbed the Church of some £100,000.

As if this were not enough, John was also suspected of murdering his nephew, Prince Arthur. Arthur, son of John's elder brother Geoffrey, died in 1186 and was regarded by many as the rightful king of England. In addition, John angered his barons by ruling like a dictator; raising heavy taxes and personally giving verdicts in the lawcourts which favoured villeins with complaints against their feudal lords.

Deer hunting was a favourite sport of medieval kings

King John grants the use of his seal on the Magna Carta at Runnymede in 1215

Even so, John might have been forgiven if only he had been victorious in battle. Instead, his wars in France lost England almost all Henry II's great empire. The barons lost patience and forced John to sign the Magna Carta: a list of their rights, privileges and land ownership (1215). They did not trust him though and invited the French Prince, Louis, to remove John from the throne. John fought back, but died (1216), soon after disaster had overtaken his army: all its equipment was lost in the Wash.

Churchmen disliked John's liking for feasts, fine clothes and luxury

King Henry III – 1216-1272

At first all went well after 9 year old Henry III succeeded his father, John, in 1216. Barons and churchmen set up a Regency and ruled for the child-king under the provisions of the Magna Carta. Then, Henry took over the government (1227) and trouble returned. For Henry stubbornly insisted on choosing his own counsellors, but not from among his barons. He preferred the foreigners who crowded to court with his French wife, Eleanor. The barons' fury grew as Henry poured money away on fruitless wars, trying to retrieve the lost lands in France, and spent vast sums on fine clothes, jewels and other fripperies for himself and his court.

The inevitable explosion came in 1258, when the barons, led by Simon de Montfort, Earl of Leicester and Henry's

brother-in-law, forced Henry to agree to the Provisions of Oxford. These included the setting up of a barons' council to advise the king. Henry was very frightened but he soon wriggled out of his promises by asking the Pope to absolve him. The barons now resorted to force. They smashed Henry's army at Lewes (1264) and took the king prisoner. Now, Henry was Simon's puppet who signed documents and issued

Both horse and rider wore chain mail for fighting or jousting. They wore surcoats over the top which came from the days of the Crusades when they were introduced to protect horse and rider from the sun

Detail of stained glass

Henry III (inset) rebuilt Westminster Abbey and created a beautiful shrine for the bones of his favourite Saint, Edward the Confessor.
The two towers seen in this modern photograph were not added until 1735

decrees as Simon demanded. Gradually the other barons grew jealous of Simon's increasing power. Led by Henry's son, Edward, they turned against Simon and defeated and killed him at the battle of Evesham (1265). Henry, free once more, had nothing more to do with government. He spent his last years working on his favourite project − rebuilding Westminster Abbey.

King Edward I, nicknamed Longshanks – 1272-1307

Edward with his Queen, Eleanor of Castile. When she died in 1290, Edward was so distraught that he erected 'Eleanor crosses' at every place her funeral cortège stopped on its way to London

Clothes of this period were simple, without much ornament but made of very beautiful materials

Tall, handsome, a splendid warrior and a wise ruler, King Edward I was like a blast of vigorous fresh air after the dismal reigns of John and Henry III. In re-establishing royal authority, stamping out corruption among tax collectors and other matters of government, Edward took care to work with the Great Council (Parliament). In 1295, he summoned for the first time, representatives of Church, barons and Commons to his *Model Parliament*. Afterwards, Edward agreed not to raise taxes without Parliament's consent.

Edward wanted to rule all Britain and that meant war against the Welsh (1277-1282) and Scots (1296-1307). Edward proved a savage conqueror in Wales, which he afterwards guarded with a ring of massive castles.

Ships at this time had castles at bow and stern for archers

The Welsh lost the last of their own princes, so Edward gave them another, one 'who would speak no English'. When his son, the future Edward II, was born in Caernarvon Castle (1282), the king 'gave' him to the Welsh: of course, the infant could not speak English – or any other language. The eldest son of an English monarch has been Prince of Wales ever since.

The Scots remained unconquered which was no small achievement considering Edward's military prowess. The size of his army included 20,000 bowmen and was the largest up to that time. Despite his failure to conquer them, Edward became known as 'the hammer of the Scots'. He was still trying to hammer them to defeat in 1307, when he died on the way to fight yet another campaign.

The rebec was a three-stringed medieval instrument made from a single piece of wood

King Edward II – 1307-1327

One terrifying night in September 1327, horrible screams were heard in the countryside around Berkeley Castle. When they faded away, Edward II, the deposed king of England was dead – brutally murdered with a red hot iron.

How did the son of the splendid King Edward I come to meet such an ignominious fate? It was his own fault.

Berkeley Castle

To Edward II, being a king meant doing as he pleased and enjoying himself. Edward had no interest in government or in the manly business of war. He preferred to spend his time with his handsome and arrogant

Edward with Piers Gaveston, gardening

Queen Isabella was nicknamed the 'She Wolf of France'

favourite, the Gascon knight, Piers Gaveston. Edward showered Gaveston with gifts and neglected his Queen, Isabella of France.

Enraged, the barons threatened Edward with rebellion if he did not banish Gaveston and restore proper government. Frightened, Edward gave in, but Gaveston soon returned, and this time, the barons got rid of him for ever: they murdered him (1312).

The distraught Edward had to wait for revenge until 1321, when his new favourites the Marcher lords, Hugh Despenser and his son, helped him break the domination of the barons.

Queen Isabella however was determined the Despensers should not humiliate her, as Gaveston had done. In 1325, Isabella went to France and joined forces with the Despensers' enemies there: one was Roger Mortimer, who became Isabella's lover. When Isabella and Mortimer returned to England with their army, the Despensers and other royal supporters were hunted down and put to death. King Edward was taken prisoner, forced to give up his throne and later met his gruesome end in Berkeley Castle.

An early form of carriage used by ladies. It was extremely uncomfortable and needed a large team of horses to pull it over rough roads. The cover was painted linen stretched over wooden hoops

King Edward III – 1327-1377

In 1330, the English once again had a king they could be proud of. In that year, 18 year old Edward III seized power from his mother, Queen Isabella and her greedy, ambitious lover, Roger Mortimer. Edward III set about creating a magnificent court ruled by ideals of chivalry and comradeship. Edward, in fact, modelled his court on the Camelot of King Arthur and his Knights of the Round Table. He enjoyed excellent relations with his barons, for Edward married several of his eleven children into baronial families, and

Edward's arms show the French fleur-de-lys, indicating his claim to the French throne. His son, Edward, was called the Black Prince because he wore black armour. Plate armour, rather than chain mail, was introduced at this time and was found to be much more effective

shared their chief interests – jousting, pageantry, hunting and, above all, war. Edward III and his much-admired son, Edward, the Black Prince, were very successful in war. So much so, that with victories like Crecy (1346) and Poitiers (1356), the English won back almost one quarter of France. It was thrilling, magnificent, and for Edward III's barons, very lucrative.

one third of the population dead. After 1364, the new king of France, Charles V, began to win back the lands King Edward III had won. By 1374, only the port of Calais and a small strip of coast in southwest France still remained in English hands. Sadder still, the Black Prince died in 1376, and his now ailing father the following year. Worst of all, the throne of England now passed to the Black Prince's son, Richard aged 10, who soon turned out to be another Edward II.

It was the skill of the English bowmen which won the Battles of Crecy and Poitiers. They were deadly marksmen up to 250 yards (228 m)

A medieval windmill. The whole structure was raised on a central post around which the mill could turn to face the wind. The sails were of linen stretched over a wooden frame

Tragically, these stirring, glorious days did not last. In 1347, the Black Death (bubonic plague) ravaged Europe and England, leaving

King Richard II –
1377-1399

Like Edward II, Richard II earned his barons' hatred by devoting himself to pleasure-loving favourites and treating the great men of his kingdom with contempt. Richard even insulted his uncle, John of Gaunt, the Duke of Lancaster, who tried to guide and advise him and protected the young king against his greedier and more ambitious barons. Richard, however, believed that kings were

Richard's splendid coronation proved too much for a ten year old and he fell asleep during it!

appointed by God and could do as they pleased. The barons refused to stand for this arrogance. So they attacked Richard by attacking his friends. At the 'Merciless'

The long war with France, and the Black Death, had made the country poor. Angry peasants marched on London and the young king met and talked to their leader, Wat Tyler. In a scuffle, Wat Tyler was killed but Richard saved the situation by promising to be the mob's leader

Dress in this period became much more elaborate

Parliament (1388) five nobles, the 'Lords Appellant', charged some of Richard's friends with treason. Those friends were hung, drawn and quartered as punishment. Richard swore revenge, bided his time, and then, in 1397, he struck. Two Appellants were arrested and the other three were exiled. One of them was Henry Bolingbroke, John of Gaunt's son.

Now Richard behaved like a mad tyrant. Anyone who caught his eye had to kneel to him and he kept a large private army to crush all opposition. Then Richard made a disastrous mistake. Gaunt died and Richard seized his lands which rightfully belonged to the exiled Henry Bolingbroke.

At once, Henry returned to England to retrieve his lands. That was what he told the barons who came to join him. In fact, Henry intended to seize Richard's throne. Richard was captured in an ambush, forced to give up his crown and was left to starve to death in Pontefract Castle (1400). Henry Bolingbroke was now King Henry IV.

THE HOUSE OF LANCASTER
Henry IV – 1399-1413

Hats and very elaborate head-dresses were typical of this period. They were called chaperons. Also, the forked beard came back in fashion

Henry IV was a most unhappy king, plagued by endless troubles: rebellion in Wales, wars in Scotland, struggles over money with Parliament, plots against his life and revolts against his rule. After one revolt, in 1400, thirty rebels were executed and their chopped-up bodies were displayed in London as an awful warning. Nevertheless, in 1403, several barons, formerly Henry's supporters, rebelled against him. One of them, the Archbishop of York, was killed. Soon afterwards, Henry was struck by a paralysing illness and people whispered that God was punishing him for killing a churchman.

The murder of the Archbishop of York

Dogs kept in the middle ages such as the mastiff, used as a guard dog, and hounds and running dogs, used for hunting

Before he became king, Henry had been a brilliant, dashing nobleman, admired throughout Europe for his chivalry. That Henry was a very different man from King Henry IV, the sickly, nervous invalid, who was constantly tormented by guilt over the murder of Richard II. Though cruel, unjust and tyrannical, Richard *had* been the rightful king. Besides, Henry was not Richard's rightful heir, but a usurper. Henry's father, John of Gaunt, was the THIRD son of King Edward III. Richard had many relatives descended from Lionel, Duke of Clarence, SECOND son of Edward III – so, they had a far better claim to be kings of England. Later, these cousins would take up arms as 'Yorkists' and fight for the throne against the 'Lancastrians' who were Henry IV's side of the family. This was the civil war known as the Wars of the Roses.

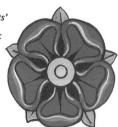

Emblems of the 'Yorkists' and 'Lancastrians'. The white rose of York and the red rose of Lancaster

45

Henry V – 1413-1422

Men's hair was worn closely cropped with the back of the neck shaved

This war, in which the English nobility ruined

The Battle of Agincourt

themselves, might have started earlier if Henry IV's son and successor had not been the magnificent warrior-king, Henry V. Henry V, who succeeded his father in 1413, stirred all England with tremendous enthusiasm when he made war in France, claiming he was the rightful king of that country. Henry was thrillingly successful. His 10,000 archers shattered the French knights at Agincourt (1415) and afterwards, the triumphant Henry forced the French King, Charles VI, to recognise him as his heir. In 1420, Henry married Charles' daughter, Catherine.

France in 1420, after the Treaty of Troyes. This made Henry V Regent of France and heir to the French throne

English

French

No English king had performed such deeds since the young Edward III. But tragedy lay not far off. In 1422, Henry V died, leaving as his heir an eight month old child, Henry VI. After 1429, the French, rallied by Joan of Arc, began to reconquer their country. By 1453, nearly everything was lost.

Much worse was to come. In 1453, King Henry VI, son and successor of Henry V, went mad. Peaceloving and religious, Henry VI had never been a strong ruler, and now his 'Yorkist' rival, Richard, Duke of York, tried to seize power. Richard was opposed by 'Lancastrian' lords who supported Henry, and the dispute exploded into civil war.

Henry VI – 1422-1461

Henry VI was crowned King of England and France but he was to lose both through violent means, which he detested

Joan of Arc was burned at the stake in Rouen

The Duke of York won the first battle, at St Albans (1455), and Henry was taken prisoner. Poor Henry, who slipped in and out of bouts of madness, was quite content to let the Duke of York rule England for him; but his stubborn, courageous Queen, Margaret, would have none of it. Determined to preserve the throne for her son, Prince Edward, Margaret gathered an army, which defeated the Yorkists at Wakefield (1460). The Duke of York was killed and Henry was rescued from prison. The Lancastrian triumph did not last long.

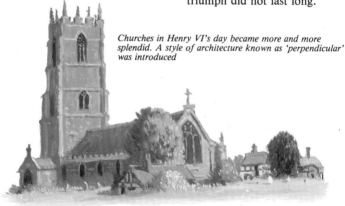

Churches in Henry VI's day became more and more splendid. A style of architecture known as 'perpendicular' was introduced

The Yorkists routed Margaret's forces at Towton (1461) and in northern England (1463). Margaret fled with her son to France. Henry VI, probably to his relief, returned to prison, in the Tower of London. Meanwhile, in June 1461, King Edward IV, son of the dead Duke of York, was crowned in Westminster Abbey.

THE HOUSE OF YORK
Edward IV – 1461-1483

Edward and his Queen, Elizabeth Woodville

Edward was nineteen, six feet tall, golden-haired, very handsome, a fine soldier and a strong and determined character. Edward made this plain when he got rid of the powerful Richard, Earl of Warwick, his cousin. In 1464, Warwick was enraged when

Edward married an Englishwoman, Lady Elizabeth Woodville, instead of the French princess he had chosen for him. Warwick turned traitor, joined forces with Queen Margaret and invaded England (1471). Warwick quickly paid for his treachery: Edward smashed his army at Barnet, where the great Earl was killed. Margaret met total disaster at Tewkesbury, where her son died. On the night Margaret arrived at the Tower as a prisoner, King Henry was murdered, possibly by Edward's brother, Richard, Duke of Gloucester.

Now that peace had returned to England, trade revived and royal authority was supreme. King Edward became rich, as a merchant in his own right, and by building up the royal estates until he owned one-fifth of England.

A 15th century sailing ship typical of those which set off to explore the unknown world

49

Edward V – 1483
Richard III – 1483-1485

Richard III was the last English king to be killed in battle

Edward IV died in April 1483, leaving his throne to his 12 year old son, Edward V. Edward V was deposed on the grounds that his parents' marriage had been illegal, and the crown was offered to Richard. Here, a mystery began. In July, young Edward's uncle, Richard, Duke of Gloucester, was crowned King Richard III. After August, Edward V and

his brother, the Duke of York, were never seen alive again. Did Richard murder them? Or were they killed by Henry Tudor, Earl of Richmond, now the Lancastrian leader? Did Richard seize the crown because a child king would not be strong enough to defend England against the Lancastrians? No one really knows. What is certain is that Richard had little hope of holding on to the throne. He was, in fact, the last king of the Plantagenet family which had ruled England since Henry II succeeded to the throne in 1154.

Richard worked hard to be a responsible ruler: he ensured the courts operated justly, he showed respect for the Church, but it was no use. Richard had too many enemies among the nobility who did not trust a ruler suspected of murdering two kings – Henry VI and Edward V. Richard's position was further weakened when his only son, Edward, died in 1484.

Then, in 1485, Henry Tudor invaded England, and Lancastrians met Yorkists at Bosworth in the last great battle of the Wars of the Roses. Richard fought

Edward and his brother in the Tower of London. In 1674 the bones of two children were found in the Tower and they are presumed to be those of the young princes

valiantly, but he was doomed when one of his nobles, Lord Stanley, deserted him and went over to Henry's side. Richard was urged to save himself by running away, but refused and fought on till he was killed.

Legend has it that Lord Stanley found Richard's crown hanging from a thornbush, and gave it to Henry Tudor, who was now the new king, Henry VII.

A fifteenth century cannon used to batter down doors and fortifications. After the Battle of Bosworth, cannons began to be used more and more

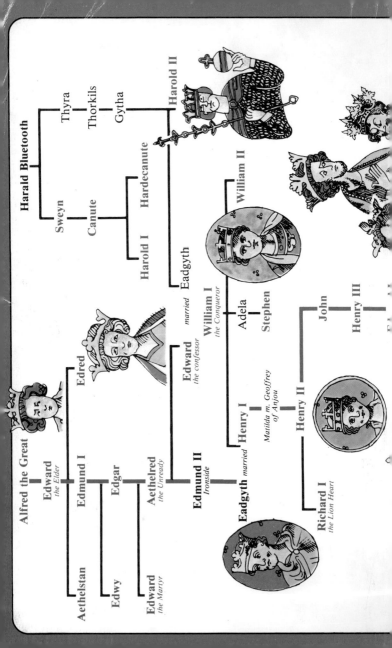

Alfred the Great

Edward *the Elder*

Aethelstan

Edmund I

Edred

Edgar

Edwy

Edward *the Martyr*

Aethelred *the Unready*

Edward *the Martyr*

Edmund II *Ironside*

Eadgyth *married*

Edward *the confessor*

Harald Bluetooth

Sweyn

Canute

Harold I

Hardecanute

Thyra

Thorkils

Gytha

Harold II

Eadgyth

William I *the Conqueror* *married*

William II

Adela

Stephen

Matilda *m. Geoffrey of Anjou*

Henry I

Henry II

Richard I *the Lion Heart*

John

Henry III